Harry came to school the next mo[...] made valentine. There was a big heart painted on it with real fingernail polish.

"I'm asking Song Lee today," he said as he walked into class.

"Asking her what?" I whispered.

"You'll see."

Harry sat there holding his valentine while Miss Mackle was reading Finocchio. He was so interested in today's episode that he didn't pass the card. Finally, the teacher stopped reading—right where the serpent laughs so loud he bursts a blood vessel.

"Eeyew, gross," I said.

"Eeyew, neat-o," Harry replied. Then he turned and handed me the valentine. "Pass this to Song Lee," he whispered.

At last! I thought. Now I could find out what Harry was up to. Quickly I read the message on the card.

Twice. I couldn't believe it the first time..

Harry wanted to marry Song Lee!

ALSO BY SUZY KLINE

Horrible Harry in Room 2B
Horrible Harry and the Green Slime
Horrible Harry and the Ant Invasion
Horrible Harry's Secret
Horrible Harry and the Christmas Surprise
Horrible Harry and the Kickball Wedding
Song Lee in Room 2B
Song Lee and the Hamster Hunt
Song Lee and the Leech Man

Herbie Jones
Herbie Jones and the Birthday Showdown
Herbie Jones and the Class Gift
Herbie Jones and the Hamburger Head
Herbie Jones and the Monster Ball
What's the Matter with Herbie Jones?
Herbie Jones and the Dark Attic

Horrible Harry
and the
Kickball Wedding

BY SUZY KLINE
Pictures by Frank Remkiewicz

PUFFIN BOOKS

Special appreciation
to Mary Ann Boulanger, my colleague and friend,
for her insight,
and
to Liz Breckinridge, my editor, for her enthusiasm
and hard work.

PUFFIN BOOKS
Published by the Penguin Group
Penguin Books USA Inc., 375 Hudson Street, New York, New York 10014, U.S.A.
Penguin Books Ltd, 27 Wrights Lane, London W8 5TZ, England
Penguin Books Australia Ltd, Ringwood, Victoria, Australia
Penguin Books Canada Ltd, 10 Alcorn Avenue, Toronto, Ontario, Canada M4V 3B2
Penguin Books (N.Z.) Ltd, 182-190 Wairau Road, Auckland 10, New Zealand

Penguin Books Ltd, Registered Offices: Harmondsworth, Middlesex, England

First published in the United States of America by Viking,
a division of Penguin Books USA Inc., 1992
Published in Puffin Books, 1995

7 9 10 8

Text Copyright © Suzy Kline, 1992
Illustrations Copyright © Frank Remkiewicz, 1992
All rights reserved

THE LIBRARY OF CONGRESS HAS CATALOGED THE VIKING EDITION AS FOLLOWS:
Kline, Suzy.
Horrible Harry and the kickballwedding/by Suzy Kline;
illustrations by Frank Remkiewicz.   p.   cm.
Summary: As Valentine's Day approaches, the students in Room 2B
are preoccupied with the kickball and a possible wedding
between Horrible Harry and Song Lee.
ISBN 0-670-83358-4
[1. Schools—Fiction. 2. Valentine's Day—Fiction.]
I. Remkiewicz, Frank, ill. II. Title.
Pz7.K6797Hnp   1992   [Fic]—dc20   92-5827   CIP   AC

Puffin Books ISBN 0-14-034453-5

Printed in the United States of America
Set in Century Schoolbook

Dedicated with (love) to my class:

Melanie Bazzano	Robert Kittredge
Ashley Colella	Diane Lapseritis
Todd Davis	Craig Lovely
Erica Duprey	Jessica Marciano
Randy Ford	Matthew Marquard
Danielle Glover	James McBurney
Mark Greco	Silvio Melo
Crystal Grenier	Nicholas Moore
Nathan Hannon	Taylor Musselman
Elizabeth Jamison	Kevin Roberts
JennyLynn Jarvis	Matthew Talbot
Jonathan Kane	Brian Wilkinson

Contents

So Why Don't You Marry It?   1

Tickle Attack!   13

Big Wedding Plans   21

Harry's True Love   33

Here Come the Brides   45

Horrible Harry and
the Kickball Wedding

So Why Don't You Marry It?

Harry sits next to me in Room 2B. He looks like any other second grader except for one thing. Harry loves to do horrible things.

The week before Valentine's Day, I didn't think anything *too* horrible could happen.

But it did.

Harry and I were looking at his new library book, *The Bug Hall of Fame*. Song Lee was looking at it too. "See that giant water bug?" she said. "When I live in Korea, I see one eat a fish."

"No fooling?" Harry flashed his white teeth at Song Lee. He's had a crush on her ever since she brought in a potato beetle for show-and-tell in kindergarten.

"Hey, Doug," Harry said.

"Yeah?" I replied.

"Look! Here's a picture of a stinkbug."

"Eeyew, neat-o!" I said.

Then he turned the page. "And a KISSING BUG!"

Just as I made a face, Mary appeared. She had a pile of bright red valentines in her hand. "Ohhhhhhh! Did you say BUGS KISS?"

Ida joined the conversation. "We

2

know they do, Mary. Remember when we had our ant farm? Ants kiss every time they pass food."

Harry lowered his bushy eyebrows. "Ants are *not* bugs—they're insects. We're talking about bugs."

"Well," Mary snapped. "They're romantic, whatever they are!"

Suddenly, Sidney peered over her shoulder. "If you love ants so much, why don't you marry one?"

"SIDNEY!" Mary shouted. "That's dumb! You can't marry an ant."

The rest of us tried not to laugh, but it was hard. Sidney's joke was so stupid, it was funny.

When the bell rang, everyone returned to their seats. Except Mary. She was still passing out her valentines.

"Mary," the teacher said. "It's too

early to pass those out. Please collect them."

Mary made a long face. "Yes, Miss Mackle."

"Boys and girls, we will pass out valentines on Thursday, when it's Valentine's Day. We will also have a party and a special Valentine's Day square dance."

Everyone cheered.

"If you can wear something with a touch of red or white in it. that would be fun," the teacher added.

"I know what I'm wearing," Harry blurted out. "My black-widow sweatshirt!"

"You're supposed to wear *Valentine* colors," Mary grumbled.

"I am!" Harry replied. "A black widow has a *touch* of red. Heh! Heh!

The deadly red hourglass."

"Eeeeeeyew!" Mary groaned.

"The black widow is poisonous," Ida said.

Miss Mackle just smiled.

Later, when we were standing in the lunch line, everyone was talking about what they would wear for Valentine's day. But not Harry and me. We were too busy taking deep whiffs.

"Mmmmmmm. It's hot dog day!" Harry said. "I love hot dogs!"

Sidney made his eyebrows go up and down. "So . . . why don't you marry one?"

This time the joke was on Harry and he didn't like it.

All through lunch he glared at Sidney. We knew that the hot dogs weren't the *only* things steaming. Harry was, too!

After lunch, our class went outside for recess. Some of us started up a kick-ball game. Harry raced for the pitcher's mound.

"I GET TO BE PITCHER!" he shouted.

Dexter ran for the plate.

"I'M UP FIRST!" he called. Then he pushed his hair back with his fingers. Ever since January when he transferred into our class, Dexter's been the king of kickball.

"I'm FIRST BASE!" Ida yelled.

"I'm SECOND!" I shouted.

After everyone took a position, Harry said, "What do you want, Dex? My slime ball . . . slow and smooth over the plate? Or my new specialty . . . *the cyclone ball?*"

Dexter rubbed his hands together.

"Gimme the cyclone!" he said as he

8

kicked the air twice with his big blue sneaker. When he stopped running his fingers through his hair, we knew he was ready for the big pitch.

Harry wound up twice and delivered a fast, bouncy ball over the plate. Dexter ran forward and gave it a hard kick.

THONK!

The ball soared high in the air to center field. It looked like a sure home run!

Dexter thought so, too. He went into his Elvis routine, rocking and rolling around the bases.

> "Be bop da-boom!
> Be bop da-boom!
> Shoogie-boogie
> Boogie-shoogie
> SLAM! BAM! BOOM!"

Then it happened. Deep in center

field, all the way back by the big
tree . . . "SHE'S GOT IT!" I screamed.

It was Song Lee! She grabbed the ball
right out of the air with both hands and
pulled it close to her chest.

"Dexter's out! Yahoo!" Harry yelled as he ran to center field and gave Song Lee a big hug.

When recess was over and we lined up, Sidney patted Harry on the back.

"You *really* love kickball, don't you?"

"Yeah!" Harry said, pointing both thumbs up.

"So why don't you marry it, then?"

Harry poked Sidney in the chest. "You like to laugh? Just wait till I tickle *your* funnybone. After school!"

As I watched Sidney duck behind the teacher, I shook my head.

Poor Sidney.

He was in for it now. Harry's revenge!

Tickle Attack!

At 3:03 P.M., I sat on the school lawn reading a book while Harry hid behind the pricker bush waiting for Sidney.

When Dexter strolled by, Harry peeked out at him. "Hey, Dex!"

Dexter took a step back. "You hiding from someone?"

"Eh . . . no. Just looking for slugs under these rocks."

"That's cool. Hey, did I get robbed or what? Man, that should have been a homer-illo."

"Yeah," Harry said. "Right-arillo! But Song Lee is an awesome player."

Dexter nodded. "Wait till I get my cousin's new soccer ball. You kick that sucker and it flies!"

"All right!" Harry said.

Then Dexter spotted me on the lawn and waved. Harry and I waved back as we watched him rock and roll up the street singing:

> "Shoogie boogie boo!
> Shoogie boogie boo!
> Boogie-shoogie
> Shoogie-boogie
> Boogity boo!"

Soon after Dexter left, Sidney came by. Harry was waiting for him.

"Aha!" he shouted as he leaped up,

wiggling his fingers. "It's time for . . .
the *tickle attack!*"

Harry jumped on Sidney.

"Hey! What are you doing?" Sidney
said as they tumbled to the ground.

"Heh! Heh! Heh!" Harry cackled.

Then he slipped his fingers inside

Sidney's jacket and started tickling his armpits.

"HA! HA! HA!" Sidney howled. "STOP! HA! HA! STOP!"

A bunch of letters fell out of Sidney's pocket when he was screaming and shaking. I thought they were probably valentines. My name was on one of them.

"Are you gonna stop bugging me about marrying hot dogs or kickballs?"

"YES! HA! HA! I PROMISE!"

As soon as Harry stopped, Sidney jumped to his feet. He looked like he was going to cry. "You know what? My . . . my . . . mom's *really* getting married Saturday."

Harry's eyes were as big as mine!

We watched Sidney pick up the letters and stuff them back in his pocket.

17

"Mom wants me to invite you guys, but I don't feel like it. I don't even want to go myself!"

"Who's your mom marrying?" I asked as I got up and closed my book.

"Some guy named George. He sells tombstones."

"Tombstones?" I asked. "That's interesting. Is he nice?"

Sidney shrugged. "He's okay. I don't know why Mom has to *marry* him. I'm supposed to be in the wedding ceremony and go to some dumb rehearsal tonight at the church. But I don't want to!"

Then Sidney started crying and ran up the street.

I shook my head. "Well, now we know why Sidney has marriage on the brain."

"Yeah," Harry said. "Too bad he isn't handing out those invitations. I love weddings. They're fun."

"They are? I've never been to one."

"You have *never* been to a wedding, Doug?"

"Nope," I said, shaking my head. "But I saw one on TV and one in a movie."

"That's not the same thing as *being* there. We've got to do something about this."

When Harry spotted Song Lee walking up the street, he suddenly snapped his fingers. "That's it! And doing it on Valentine's Day would be perfect!"

"Doing . . . what?"

"You'll see, Doug." Then he flashed his big toothy smile. "First, I have to pick up a few things at the party store, and then I need to borrow some of Mom's red fingernail polish."

What was Harry up to? I couldn't wait to find out!

Big Wedding Plans

Harry came to school the next morning with a special homemade valentine. There was a big heart painted on it with red fingernail polish.

"I'm asking Song Lee today," he said as he walked into class.

"Asking her what?" I whispered.

"You'll see."

Harry sat there holding his valentine while Miss Mackle was reading *Pinocchio*. He was so interested in today's episode that he didn't pass the card. Finally, the teacher stopped reading—right where the serpent laughs so loud he bursts a blood vessel.

"Eeyew, gross," I said.

"Eeyew, neat-o," Harry replied. Then he turned and handed me the valentine. "Pass this to Song Lee," he whispered.

At last! I thought. Now I could find out what Harry was up to. Quickly I read the message on the card.

Twice. I couldn't believe it the first time.

Harry wanted to marry Song Lee!

A few minutes later, a note came back. I decided *not* to unfold it. Song Lee's answer was private. Besides, I figured I could tell what Song Lee said just by watching Harry when he read the note.

But I couldn't.

Harry didn't blink while he was reading it. He didn't put his head down on his desk and he didn't smile. He just looked at the clock.

What did Song Lee say?

I didn't find out until lunch recess. Harry rounded up me and Sidney, and then we found Song Lee playing hopscotch with Ida and Mary by the dumpster. Harry said it was okay for Mary and Ida to listen too.

"Song Lee," he said. "Do you want to get married on Valentine's Day?"

"Ohh!" Mary sighed. "How romantic!"

"Harry," Song Lee said, "I tell you in my note. We are not grown-up. My aunt get married last summer but she was twenty-two. I am just seven and a half now."

Harry shrugged. "So? I'm eight and I've been to *three* weddings. We could have our own ceremony, ourselves!"

"We could?" Song Lee replied.

"Sure," Harry said. "I just have to check with Sidney on a few details. How was that wedding rehearsal last night?"

Everyone stared at Sidney.

"*Whose* wedding rehearsal?" Mary asked.

Sidney kicked a piece of chalk on the blacktop. "My mom's," he grumbled.

"YOUR MOTHER IS GETTING MARRIED?"

Sidney groaned. "Unfortunately."

"That's so exciting!" Mary exclaimed. "What do you do in the wedding?"

"I'm the ring bearer. I carry the ring down the aisle on a little pillow and then I stand near the minister."

"That's neat," Ida replied.

"Hey, Sid," Harry said. "Can you remember some of the words your minister says and say them for Song Lee and me?"

Sidney shrugged. "If you want me to, I guess I can."

Everyone looked at Mary. She was usually the one who organized things.

"I couldn't be the minister," Mary said. "I've never been to a wedding before."

I smiled. I was glad I wasn't the only one.

Sidney stopped grumbling. I think he liked being in charge for a change. "Well, where do you want to have the ceremony?"

Harry looked at the big tree on the playground. There was a squirrel running across the branches. "Hey, how about by the tree, Thursday morning?"

"I remember tree the first day of second grade," Song Lee giggled.

"Me too," I said. "That's where Harry trapped you with his garter snake."

"Heh! Heh! Heh!" Harry chuckled. "Just being friendly."

Mary put her nose in Harry's face. "No snakes in this wedding ceremony!"

"*Okay!*" Harry said, putting his hands up. Then he lowered his voice.

"How about a couple of bugs?"

"Only if they're not real," Mary scolded.

"You want bogus bugs?" Harry replied. "You get bogus bugs."

For the next ten minutes Sidney helped us make our big wedding plans. When we were finished, he said, "Well, Song Lee, now I know that Harry would rather marry *you* than a hot dog or a kickball."

Everyone laughed except Harry.

"I was just kidding!" Sidney explained.

Harry made a half smile. "Well, did we forget anything?"

Song Lee nodded. "I think I should ask Mother first. If she gives me permission, then I marry you, Harry."

Harry dropped to his knees like he

was praying. "Pleeeeease say yes!"

I couldn't believe it.

On Valentine's Day, I might be going to my first wedding.

HARRY'S!

Harry's True Love

Wednesday morning when it was our turn to use the art table, Song Lee told us what her mother said.

"It is okay to pretend we get married. Mother is making me veil out of old lacy white curtain from . . . bathroom." Then she giggled.

Harry socked the air. "Yahoo!"

Sidney cut something out of brown construction paper and taped it under his nose. "Now do I look like a minister?"

"With that mustache," I said, "you look more like Groucho Marx."

"Very funny, Doug."

"No, I like it! Do you have any good ideas for me? What does the best man wear?"

"A boutonniere."

"A boo-tin-what?"

"Boutonniere," Sidney repeated. "That's a white carnation."

"I can show you how to make one, Doug," Mary said. "Just get me some Kleenex."

As we worked at the art table, Mary and Ida made daisies out of yellow and orange construction paper for their bridesmaid bouquets. Song Lee made some insects out of folded paper and glued them on her wedding bouquet.

"That's neat," Harry said.

"It is origami," Song Lee said. "Japanese paper folding. I show you how to make grasshopper."

Miss Mackle came over and asked us

what we were doing. Song Lee giggled, Harry shrugged, and I just smiled. None of us wanted to tell the teacher. "Looks like fun," Miss Mackle said.

The next morning at 8:30 A.M. we all met by the big tree.

Song Lee looked beautiful! She was wearing a red sweater with white fuzzy hearts on it. The bathroom curtain on her head looked just like a wedding veil!

Mary examined the bogus bugs on Harry's boutonniere. "A black-widow and a lady bug. Ohh! My goodness!"

Harry grinned.

Sidney fiddled with his paper mustache but he couldn't get it dead center under his nose.

"I didn't bring our family Bible," he said, "because it's too heavy. I just brought another black book. See?"

We all read the title of Sidney's book: *Easy Car Repairs.*

I felt like *I* was twenty-two standing

there next to Harry with my Kleenex boutonniere. "You hold this," he whispered as he handed me a peanut can.

"The wedding ring's inside?" I whispered.

"It sure is," Harry grinned.

I wondered why the can didn't rattle. Even a plastic ring would make some noise.

While Sidney double-checked to see if we were standing in the right places, Ida and Mary started singing a song they had made up, to the tune of "She'll Be Comin' Round the Mountain":

"O-oh, Harry's getting married to
   Song Lee,
   O-oh, Harry's getting married to
   Song Lee.
   There will be a big, big wedding

By the tree where we go
   sledding,
O-oh, Harry's getting married to
   Song Lee!"

Sidney cleared his throat. "I memorized the words for this special Valentine wedding ceremony."

"Good going, Sid," Harry said as he took Song Lee's hand.

"Ohhh," Mary sighed. "True love."

Sidney opened up his black book to the chapter called "Oil, Lube and Filter," and began his speech.

"Dearly beloved, we are gathered together in front of the big tree and these witnesses to bring together Song Lee and Harry in marriage . . . through sickness and health . . . and . . . "

Just then Dexter walked by and gave

us this weird look. He was bouncing a
new soccer ball. "Who wants to play a
game of *real* kickball?"

Harry's head slowly turned as he
watched Dexter run to the kickball diamond with two big third graders.

When Sidney asked, "Do you . . .

Harry, take Song Lee to be your wife,"
Harry wasn't listening anymore.

He was unpinning his boutonniere.

"Well?" Sidney said. "Do you?"

"Eh . . . I'll see you guys later," Harry
mumbled. Then he took off!

Mary's eyes bulged. "Where's he
going?"

"To the kickball diamond," I said.

"KICKBALL!" Mary and Ida shouted
together.

"He's supposed to say, 'I do,' " said
Sidney.

"HOW HORRIBLE!" Ida exclaimed.
"Poor Song Lee! Deserted at the altar!"

Suddenly Song Lee threw her veil in
the air and called, "Wait for me! I play
center field."

We all just stood there shaking our
heads and thinking the same thing.

Here we were at a wedding with *no* bride and *no* groom.

"Great!" Mary groaned. "Some wedding!"

Here Come
the Brides

Sidney closed his big black book, and I picked up the veil. Mary and Ida glared at the kickball diamond.

"I can't believe it," Mary said. "After all our big wedding plans!"

Slowly, Sidney reached into his back pocket.

"You want to go to a *real* wedding?"

"YES! Your mother's!" Mary and Ida said, jumping up and down.

Sidney handed each of us one of his wrinkled invitations that he had been carrying in his back pocket all week.

"Thanks, Sidney!" I said. "I really do want to see a wedding from beginning to end."

Mary put her nose in the air. "You aren't giving Harry and Song Lee *their* invitations, are you? They walked out on us."

"You mean *ran* out on us," Ida said.

Sidney nodded, "Yeah, but I know how they feel. I didn't want to be in Mom's wedding rehearsal either."

When the bell rang and everyone lined up, Sidney handed out the rest of his invitations.

Harry ripped his open. "ALL RIGHT! I wouldn't miss a wedding for any-thing!"

Mary gritted her teeth. "Except your own!"

Harry laughed as he gave the soccer ball a knuckle noogie.

"Harry," I said.

"Yeah, Doug?"

"Ol' Sid was right. You *should* have married a kickball."

Then I tossed Song Lee's veil on the ball, and Sidney started singing:

"Here comes the bride
Big, fat, and wide
Harry will marry
A kickball . . . *all right!*"

While everyone was cracking up, Harry grabbed the peanut can out of my hand. "Well, if I *am* marrying this kickball, I better get out the wedding ring."

Suddenly, everyone turned pin quiet. Our mouths dropped open as we watched Harry *slowly* take off the lid.

SCHHHHNNICK!! A huge green

python popped out of the can and went flying up into the air.

"*AAAUUUUGH!*" everyone shrieked.

Song Lee giggled while Harry howled.

When the python landed on Mary's head, she threw it back at Harry. "A cotton slinky!"

"Like it?" Harry grinned. "I got that at the party store too."

Everyone groaned.

Mary put her hands on her hips. "Harry, we've had enough of your surprises." Then she stomped into the school with Ida and Sidney.

Song Lee was still standing on the steps when Harry reached into his back pocket and pulled out a black plastic spider ring. I noticed it had a touch of bright red fingernail polish on it. When Harry slipped the ring on

Song Lee's finger, she smiled.

Not too many of us knew that Harry *did* marry Song Lee on Valentine's Day.

Just Harry, Song Lee, me, and Dexter, who sang:

> "Here comes the bride
> All red and white
> Song Lee and Harry
> Are married—*all right!*
> Boogity shoogity
> Shoogity boogity
> Be bop da-boom!"